Santa
SLEPT iN!

Crystal Paparone-Donadio

PAGE PUBLISHING, INC.
New York, NY

First originally published by Page Publishing, Inc. 2018

ISBN 978-1-63568-436-0 (Paperback)
ISBN 978-1-63568-435-3 (Hardcover)
ISBN 978-1-63568-437-7 (Digital)

Printed in the United States of America

To the children of the world,

especially D3

Enjoy!

-Cuphf

It had been a very busy year indeed.

Santa had helped the elves almost every day this year because there were so many more good boys and girls on the nice list than ever before. He wanted to make sure all the toys that were going to the children were perfect. Santa made sure the tires on the toy cars were on correctly, made sure the doll houses were sturdy, and even helped sew the button eyes on the dolls and teddy bears. Secretly, Santa also enjoyed playing with all these wonderful toys.

After working all day long, Santa, Mrs. Claus, and the elves sat down to a Christmas Eve feast together. Santa helped himself to a piece of honey-glazed ham, some macaroni and cheese, broccoli and carrots, brussels sprouts, and mashed potatoes. He washed it down with a tall glass of ice-cold milk and sneaked just one chocolate chip cookie. Santa let out a great, big yawn when he was finished. "I'm so tired I could take a catnap!" exclaimed Santa to Mrs. Claus. "Please wake me in one hour's time." Santa never napped on Christmas Eve! Santa went off to his bedroom and plopped onto his bed.

Mrs. Claus and the elves returned to the workshop to ready the sleigh and reindeer. Santa had a busy night ahead. This year, Santa would visit almost five trillion homes.

But all that hard work and preparation caught up to Santa, even though he had tons of help from the elves and Mrs. Claus this Christmas season. Almost three hours had passed, and Mrs. Claus forgot to wake Santa! When she tried to wake Santa, he just pulled the covers over his head. Mrs. Claus figured she would give him a few more minutes. She got into bed to rest herself, put on the evening news, and fell off to sleep.

Santa and Mrs. Claus woke up feeling refreshed. Santa had a jolly pep in his step and offered to make a delightful breakfast of blueberry pancakes, eggs, and bacon. As Santa whistled his way around the kitchen, he noticed the reindeer outside the kitchen window with the sleigh full of toys!

Santa yelled, "I slept in!" Mrs. Claus came running into the kitchen. "What am I going to do?" cried Santa. Mrs. Claus thought long and hard and suggested that Santa broadcast an apology to the children around the world. Santa was puzzled. "But will the children forgive me?"Mrs. Claus reminded Santa that the true meaning of Christmas is spending time with those you love. Even though Mrs. Claus's words were true, Santa wanted to make it right for all the children of the world.

Santa thought that broadcasting an apology was the best way to explain what happened. Santa hurried off to his office, turned on his computer, and broadcasted his apology with tear-filled eyes.

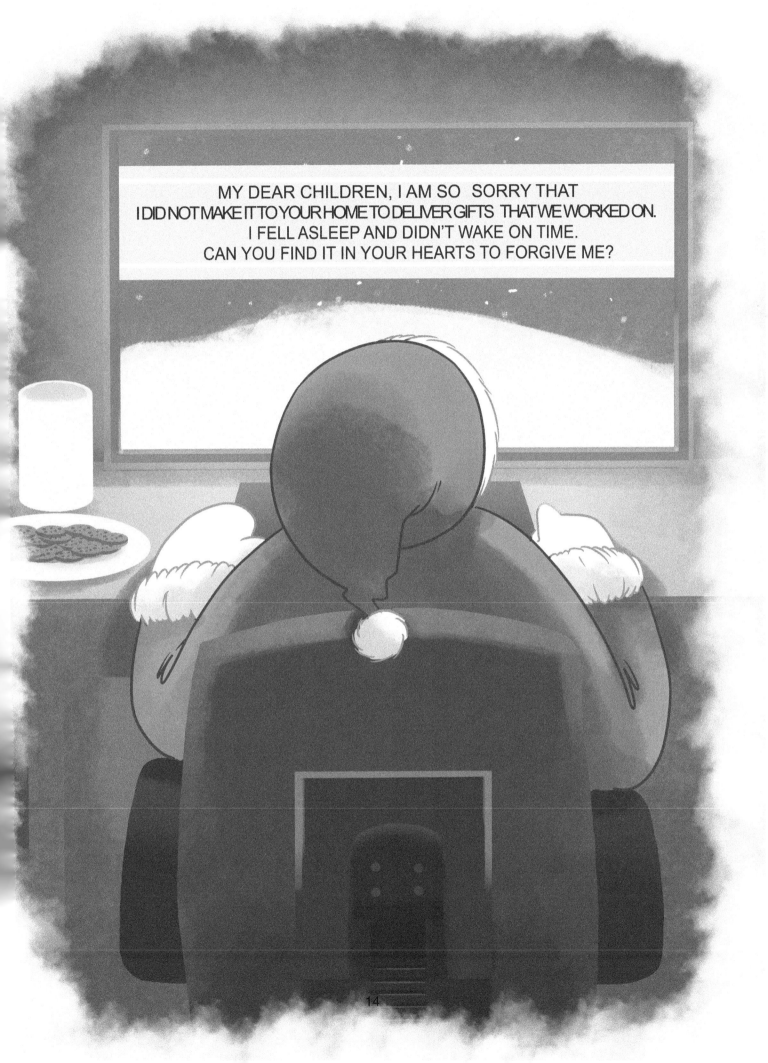

Somewhat satisfied with his message, Santa spoke to his toy department a few minutes later to discuss the best way to bring the magic of Christmas to each family. The elves brainstormed and encouraged Santa to leave on the sleigh tonight to bring the magic of Christmas to the children around the world. Santa was resistant at first but thought it over and decided that the children would really be surprised.

After lunch, Santa and Mrs. Claus prepared the sleigh for takeoff. Santa left about two hours earlier than he normally would to give himself plenty of time. Santa was feeling much better now because seeing smiling children meant the world to him!

Cries of joy were heard around the world as
the children woke up to see their goodies.
Santa had not let the children down!

Santa made it back home in time to see their delight in his Smile-O-Meter crystal ball. It was such a perfect moment.

Mrs. Claus entered Santa's office to see one jolly and happy Santa. Mrs. Claus offered a snack of milk and chocolate chip cookies as Santa marveled at the happy children. Santa thanked Mrs. Claus and thoroughly enjoyed his snack. Santa then looked up to Mrs. Claus and vowed to set an alarm should he ever nap on Christmas Eve again!

The End

About The Author

Santa Slept In! is Crystal's first publication. Crystal received her master's degree in education from Long Island University and works as a child and family counselor. She has worked with children and families for over ten years.

Crystal lives in New York with her husband, her son, and her dog named Chip. She enjoys traveling, reading, baking, and spending time with her family. Crystal has always loved the magic of the Christmas season and hopes to visit the North Pole one day.

Let's keep in touch! Please like the *Santa Slept In!* page on Facebook @santasleptinbook.

CPSIA information can be obtained
at www.ICGtesting.com
Printed in the USA
BVHW02s0610241018
531065BV00006B/22/P